For **Joshua,**
the archetypal bold boy
~**M.D.**

For **Dish** and **Keith**
~**J.R.**

First published 2001 by Walker Books Ltd
87 Vauxhall Walk, London SE11 5HJ

1 2 3 4 5 6 7 8 9 10

Text © 2001 Malachy Doyle
Illustrations © 2001 Jane Ray

This book has been typeset in
Futura Bold and Binner Poster

Printed in Italy

British Library Cataloguing in Publication Data:
a catalogue record for this book is available from the British Library

ISBN 0-7445-7571-0

# THE Bold Boy

written by **Malachy Doyle**

illustrated by **Jane Ray**

**WALKER BOOKS**
AND SUBSIDIARIES
LONDON • BOSTON • SYDNEY

# A bold boy

found a pea and he put it
in his nut-brown bag.

**T**hen he did a little dance
and he sang a little song
and off he toddled.

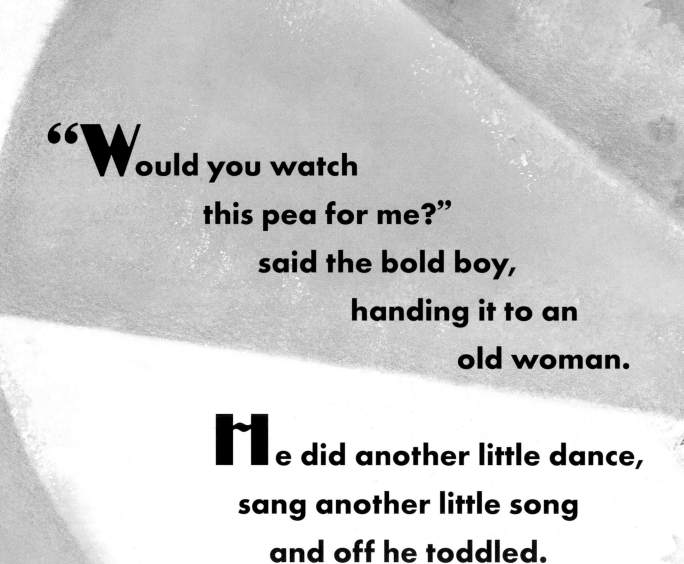

"**W**ould you watch
this pea for me?"
said the bold boy,
handing it to an
old woman.

**H**e did another little dance,
sang another little song
and off he toddled.

**T**he woman put
the pea in a bucket,
to keep it safe for
the bold boy.

**B**ut a speckledy hen
came into the kitchen.
She saw the pea and,
quick as a flash, she ate it.

"I've come for my pea," said the bold boy.
"I'm sorry to say it's been eaten,"
said the old woman.
"By whom?" said the bold boy.
"My speckledy hen that's standing there.
She's the one who ate it."

"**Naughty, naughty!**"
cried the bold boy, grabbing a-hold
of the speckledy hen and popping her
into his nut-brown bag. "You ate my pea
so now you're mine, for that's
the law where I come from!"

Then he picked up the bag
and off he toddled.

"**W**ill you keep an eye on my hen for me?" said the bold boy, handing her to an old man in the next village.

**T**hen he did a little dance and he sang a little song and off he toddled.

**S**o the old man made
a pen for the little speckled hen,
and he put her inside.

**P**iggy came to visit
and he frightened Speckled Hen.

**S**he squeaked and squawked,
she flapped her wings,
and over the hill she flew.

"**W**here's my hen?" said the bold boy.

"Frightened away," said the old man.

"**By whom?**" said the bold boy.

"My curious pig," said the old man.

"**Naughty, naughty!**" cried the bold boy,
popping the pig in his nut-brown bag.

"You're mine, you lump," said he to the pig,

"for that's the law where I come from."

**T**he pig was big, but the boy
was bold and off he jolly
well toddled.

"**W**ould you keep an
eye on my pig for me?"
he asked a young girl
in the next village.

**T**he young girl smiled
and said she would.

**S**o he did a little dance
and he sang a little song
and off he toddled.

The poor old pig was tired,
so he curled up in the stable.
But Donkey didn't want
to have a piggy in his bed.
"Ee-haw, ee-haw," he brayed
in Piggy's earhole.

The sleepy pig was
terrified and scarpered
down the lane.

"**W**here's my pig?" said the bold boy.

"Chased away," said the young girl.

"**By whom?**" said the bold boy.

"My lovely donkey," said the young girl.

"**Naughty, naughty!**"
cried the bold boy. "Your donkey's mine now,
for that's the law where I come from."

**A**nd up he jumped
and off he galloped.

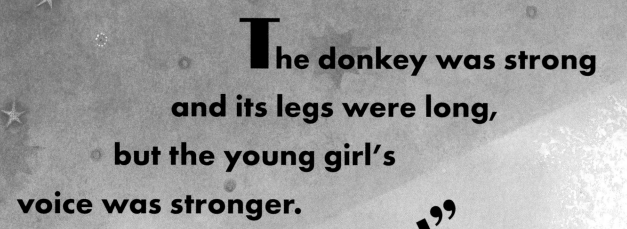

The donkey was strong
and its legs were long,
but the young girl's
voice was stronger.

"Stop!" she hollered, and
the donkey stopped.

The boy flew off
and up and over,
head first into a haystack.

"Naughty!"

The girl came running,
the man came running,
the woman came running,
each of them shouting,

"You're the one who's naughty,
stealing a hen and a pig and a donkey.
Make yourself scarce,
you naughty boy, for that's
the law round here!"

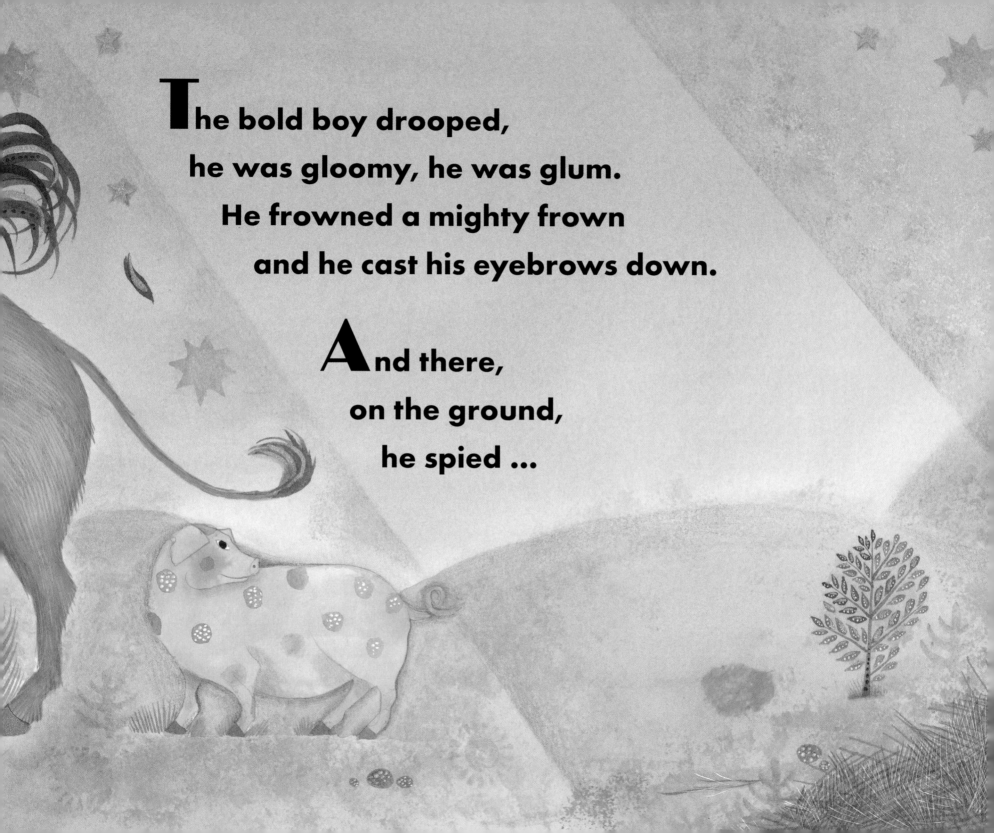

The bold boy drooped,
he was gloomy, he was glum.
He frowned a mighty frown
and he cast his eyebrows down.

And there,
on the ground,
he spied ...

a pea!

**H**e whooped
and he scooped
and he popped
it in his bag.

**T**hen he did a little dance
and he sang a little song
and off he toddled.